CW00821030

Mason and the Magic Controller

By Suzanna Salter
Illustrated by
Stephanie Blake

MASON AND THE MAGIC CONTROLLER

© SUZANNA SALTER, 2023

ILLUSTRATIONS

© STEPHANIE BLAKE

DESIGN BY LISA BRUM & KERRY MEARS

A Promise

Cross my heart
Hope to fly
Stick a cupcake
in my eye
Thank you to
Paigey Picklepants

MASON AND THE MAGIC CONTROLLER

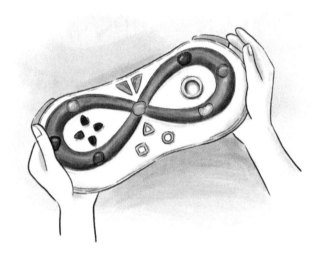

By Suzanna Salter

CONTENTS

Chapter 1
MASON

Mason was an ordinary boy, as ordinary as any other, except he had the most extraordinary smile.

If one smile could change the world, then Mason's would be the one. Mason had lived in the U.K. all his life, which might sound like a long time, but he was only 11. His family had just moved all the way to America, which as you can imagine was going to be a considerable change to such a young boy. Mason was feeling a little sad and lonely, as he had to leave all his old friends behind. The new school he was to attend had broken up for the summer, so Mason had not met or made any new friends yet.

It was such a lonely time for Mason. Mason was small for his age, but, what he lacked in stature, he made up for in heart, kindness and courage. He had a birthday coming up soon. Mason would normally have a party with all his friends, but as we know, he did not have any right now. The boy had asked for a games console every Christmas and Birthday for as long as he could remember. His parents had always refused saying "Maybe when you're older son."

However, his parents had decided that, with the move to America being such a huge change, and with Mason being so brave, during all the upheaval, that this year would be the one that his dream would come true! His parents had worked all

the overtime they could to help with the cost of the move, but they also made sure that some of the money was put aside for their son's birthday present. There was still a week until Mason's birthday, but his parents decided to cheer their son up. They would buy him his gift early as a surprise.

As they walked him into the town centre, Mason had no clue where he was going.

His parents had only said "a surprise," What could it be? He wondered. Mason hoped it was a milkshake, chocolate being his most favourite flavour in the whole world!

Imagine the surprise on his face when the family of three walked into "Gaming Galore," a computer and gaming shop! As the door opened a bell made a tinkling sound from overhead, letting whoever owned the shop know that they had a customer.. Behind the counter sat an old man. He had on a pair of glasses that kept sliding down his nose. It did not matter how many times the glasses were pushed back up they would just sllllliiiiiiiiiiiiiddddddddeeeeee back down again, his wrinkled sad eyes peering over the top of these very slippery spectacles. What hair the shopkeeper had (as there was not that much of it), was fluffy and white, looking like clouds floating just above his ears.

Mason stared wide-eyed at all the wonderful consoles and games, his heart pitter pattering with excitement. As he was walking around this wonderland of entertainment, his eyes fell upon the little old man sitting behind his counter. He had the saddest eyes that Mason had ever seen. He decided he would like to try and cheer the old man up.

Walking boldly over to the counter, he stared deep into the man's eyes and said "Hello, my name is Mason." He then gave a smile, a brilliant smile, an extraordinary smile, in fact it was the best smile Mason had ever given. The shopkeeper looked up at the beaming boy and something very strange began to happen to him. Something the old man had not done in a very long time. The sides of his mouth began to twitch, then they slowly began to curl upwards. It was such a curious feeling to him, he wanted to thank Mason for helping him to smile again by giving the boy a special gift.

He asked Mason to wait a moment and shuffled through a
doorway that had been hidden from view by an old musty

curtain. Mason's parents had been watching this exchange from afar. They came to stand beside Mason curious to see where the old man had gone. As the trio stood patiently at the counter, they could hear banging, dragging and knocking sounds coming from beyond the doorway. Eventually the old man came back. He had a bead of perspiration rolling down his forehead, he had to stand with his hand on the counter for a moment to catch his breath. The old man placed a box onto the counter, leant down towards Mason and said "Young man, I would like to thank you for helping me to remember my smile, I felt as though I would never smile again!" The shopkeeper slid the box he had brought from the back towards Mason "Please take this gift as a token of my gratitude." Mason could not believe his eyes! The old man was giving him a games console, the very thing he had been dreaming of for so long. "Thank you," whispered Mason in awe of this most wonderful of gifts.

Mason's parents thanked the shopkeeper too, asking if they might be able to pay for the console, but the shopkeeper would not hear of it, insisting this was his gift for such an amazing boy. The shopkeeper stared off into space while saying "He reminds me so much of my granddaughter," a sadness descending upon his face for a moment. He shook himself from his thoughts and smiled sadly at the family as they took their leave after thanking the old man one last time. "I wonder if I did the right thing" he mumbled to himself as he watched the family leave. "Maybe I should have warned them," he scratched his head, pondering. Eventually he nodded saying "Yes, yes I am sure I did," and shuffled off to make himself a nice warm drink, smiling and daydreaming about his granddaughter.

Chapter 2
MARISSA AND ALAN

Alan was Marissa's grandfather, he was also the owner of "Gaming Galore" a shop that sold computers and games consoles. Alan and Marissa spent every spare moment together, the love they had for each other was unbreakable. When Alan was in his shop Marissa would not be far away, apart from when school was open, they spent time walking in the park, laughing and talking about anything and everything. Marissa especially liked to hear stories about Alan from his younger years.

Alan loved to watch Marissa as she fed the ducks, giggling when they dunked their heads under the water, their feathery bottoms wiggling on top. Alan could think of no better company than his granddaughter. She made his days just that little bit more. A little bit more fun, a little bit more exciting and a little bit of him felt younger when he was around her. Because of this Alan began calling Marissa his "Little Bit." Alan always felt as though he could walk a little bit more, work a little bit more, well, you get the picture. Sadly all that changed one weekend when Alan had to go to his shop to do some stock taking.

Marissa would normally go with him, but she had not been feeling very well. She decided it was best to stay at home, in bed playing on her game console. Her grandfather agreed that bed was the best place for Marissa, he promised that once he was done in the shop he would come back and check on her. Little did he know that he would not be seeing her, because when he got home Marissa was nowhere to be found. No-one knew for sure what had happened, there were no signs of a break in. The police suggested that maybe she had run away from home. Alan knew this was not true, he knew in his heart of hearts that his "Little Bit" would never purposely leave him. Alan's search for Marissa was exhausting, his eyes blurry with tiredness and his feet throbbing with pain. Weeks then months passed but he never stopped searching.

Something was bothering Alan though, he knew Marissa would not leave of her own accord and felt deep down that he was looking in all the wrong places for her, he would sit late into the night pondering on where she might be and hoping she was safe. The truth of the matter is Marissa had been sitting in her room playing a game called "The Enchanted Forest." She was happily playing , enjoying solving the puzzles and completing levels when suddenly…

she was gone! From the moment Marissa went missing, Alan felt his life would never be the same. There were two reasons he carried on. The first was the feeling he would see Marissa again, the second was his little shop "Gaming Galore".
Alan felt it was his duty to keep his shop open, as though an unknown force was making him keep it open. He loved to see the childrens faces when they picked out a console or a game that they had been wanting. Alan loved his shop almost as much as he loved Marissa.

Alan opened every morning (apart from Sundays) without fail, taking his position behind the counter to wait patiently for any customers that might call in. During that time he would dream about finding Marissa, hugging her, laughing with her and feeling complete again. Oh what a wonderful day that would be!

Chapter 3
THE BEGINNING

When Mason and his family returned from the shopping trip, he asked them excitedly if he might be able to go and play on his new console. Both parents exchanged glances and laughed in agreement, they turned back to Mason and nodded their consent. It was all Mason needed to see before running to his bedroom with his game and console in his arms.

After making sure that the console was set up correctly, he noticed that his controller was unusually round, it had some indentations surrounding a funny sideways 8.

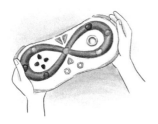

Mason began to look through the games his parents had purchased, along with the ones that came with the old man's gift.

One game in particular caught his eye. The cover was colourful and vibrant, it showed trees with birds roosting in them, lots of animals eating or playing, it appeared like the animals could see him, were staring at him through the cover of the game. Mason shook his head and laughed off the strange feeling he was getting from the cover. He decided this was the game he wanted to play first, level one was a fairly simple exercise he had to forage for food. Level two he cleared leftover nets from a river to save the fish. As Mason continued to play a message popped up telling him that if he wished to continue to "The Enchanted Forest"

he must enter a code. Mason could not remember seeing any code on the packaging, he searched through the cover looking for one. As he was looking, he heard, what sounded like, strange whispers coming from the forest on the screen. A strange static noise began and the screen went all crackly. A boy appeared on the screen. He was a young boy, maybe a little older than Mason, very long legs and a slim face. Could this have been the source of the whispering? The boy asked "Are you brave enough to enter "The Enchanted Forest", only the most courageous will survive."

Maybe it was the boy's voice that filled Mason with excitement or the thought of a thrilling quest that made him enter the code without a second thought. The controller began to vibrate, lights flashing. The next thing Mason knew he was standing in what looked to be the forest from the game he had just been playing! How could this be? Was he dreaming? Did it have something to do with the code he just used?

Dear Reader, I can confirm that, yes indeed, it was the code that had done this. As unknown to Mason, someone had created it to lure in unsuspecting children. I dare not reveal this code for fear that the same fate would happen to you!

The voice had told Mason he needed to explore. As he walked along a pathway, it appeared as though the tree branches were waving to him, even though there was no breeze to make them move. The flowers along the path were all bent over, nodding their heads as if to bid him a "Good Morning." Mason kept on walking, looking for any sign of life or clues as to what he should do next. Out of the corner of his eye he saw a flash of red. It was a robin, Mason had never seen a robin as close as this before. Imagine his shock when the bird gently landed on his shoulder. The boy gave out a faint gasp. "Sir, do you think you could possibly help me please?" Mason looked around to see where this voice had come from, he rubbed his eyes and shook his head in amazement when he realised the question had come from the bird perching upon his shoulder.

The robin asked Mason for help in clearing a tree that he and his family lived in. The tree was being smothered, slowly dying from the ivy that had taken root all around the tree. How could Mason refuse a talking robin?!

The bird flew back and forth waiting patiently for the boy to catch up and follow him. Eventually, the pair arrived at the robin's ivy laden home. The tree was completely covered from root to rip, Mason could see this was going to be a long and arduous job, but he was fully prepared for the task in hand. The boy worked hard, tugging and pulling at the ivy. The robins kept him company singing songs of encouragement to their helper.

As Mason climbed further up the tree, he spotted several

nests, each of which had pale blue robin eggs in them. The robin explained that they liked to roost in groups and so the tree was home to several families. Mason carefully cleared the Ivy from around the nests as he did not want a single nest or egg to be harmed. Finally after what felt like, (and probably was) hours, the tree was cleared. The robins swooped and sang with delight, celebrating joyously, whilst Mason sat at the base of the tree resting with a smile of satisfaction on his face of a job well done. One of the robins swooped down and sat beside Mason. He had something in his beak, the bird hopped onto Mason's leg and dropped the item into his lap. "Please keep this pebble safe Master Mason, as you will surely need it later."

Mason reached out, gently stroking the birds' head whilst thanking him for the gift. The robin added "If you ever need help from us, just whistle," Mason had so many questions to ask, but the robin flew up into the tree to check on his family leaving Mason alone with the pebble. It was the most vibrant red he had ever seen. Heeding the robins' words, he placed it into his pocket for safe keeping.

Chapter 4
HUGO

Hugo was a chubby faced boy, with ginger curly hair, braces and glasses. He was big for his age, some boys at school picked on him because of this. Bullies like to pick on people that are different in some way. Hugo was different in so many ways that he never stood a chance. Although Hugo was big, he was a gentle giant. All he wanted was for people to like him. He hated the bullies so much that he began spending less and less time playing outside and more time in his bedroom playing on his console.

Hugo went through so many emotions. Sad for being picked on, angry, hurt, cowardly for not standing up for himself. He spent a lot of time crying in his bedroom, not that he would ever let his tormentors see him shed a single tear, he would never give them that kind of satisfaction. The boy would fill his pockets with food before heading to his bedroom, he liked to make sure he could eat while playing his games. This was his daily routine now, he would come home from school and head straight up to his room with food hanging out of his pockets, food had become his coping mechanism. He was contemplating trying to make friends with the bullies.

His mum had told him that he should feel sorry for them because they felt insecure, and their home life maybe was not as good as his. Hugo was finding what his mother was saying very hard to believe, but he also trusted that his mother was only trying to do the best for him. Hugo was deep in thought about the bullies that he really was not paying attention to the game, so when it asked him to enter a code to continue, he automatically entered it. Before he could even blink his eyes he was standing in a forest.

He took a moment, sat beside a tree, dug around in his pocket for food, unwrapped a chewy bar while he pondered his problem. Where was he? Munch, chew, munch How did he get there? Chew, much, chew As he munched and chewed away he thought he had heard a voice off in the distance. "Hello," said the voice. Hugo was scared, he did not know whether to run and hide or reply. As Hugo was trying to decide on his best course of action, a small boy began to walk towards him, appearing from behind some bushes. Would this be someone else who would bully him?

Upon closer inspection the small boy was smiling. It felt like a kind, sincere smile to Hugo, he returned the smile with a huge cheesy grin.
"Hi, I'm Mason."
"I'm Hugo" he replied, "how did I get here?" "How do I get home?" "What are we meant to do?" came the barrage of questions, none of which Mason could answer. The pair

decided they felt safer walking together. Maybe they would be able to find some kind of clue as to why they were both in the strange yet wonderful place. The boys were getting hungry, so they decided to look for something to eat and a shady place to rest.

They could then put their heads together and maybe come up with a plan of action. After a short while Mason spotted an apple tree.

They both gathered an armful each and ate, whilst Mason told Hugo about his experience with the robins, the tree and the

gift of a red pebble. The pair were wondering what adventures lay ahead of them. They felt it could be a long journey. As they sat resting, contemplating their next move, they saw a strange looking animal shuffling along, its mouth full of twigs.

Chapter 5
THE BEAVERS AND
THE DAM

Hugo and Mason stared at the strange creature, its reddish brown fur shimmering in the sunlight. The boys could see a flat tail being dragged along like a miniature surfboard riding along the grass. The creature spotted the boys and wandered over on its webbed feet.

"Hello," said the creature.

"Umm hi," replied Mason

"What are you?!" asked Hugo rather rudely.

The beaver laughed a little unaffected by the question. "Why I am a beaver of course! I am here to collect items for our dam, would you like to help?" he asked.

The boys looked slightly confused. They had never seen a dam before so feeling curious as to what it might be they agreed to help. "You do know that we just talked with an animal right?" exclaimed Hugo.

"Oh I know, I have already chatted with a robin, remember?" Mason looked at Hugo and continued in a quiet voice. "I feel certain there will be more surprises." As the duo followed behind the beaver he explained that beavers need to collect almost anything that would fit into gaps in the dam, sticks, rocks, mud, grass, leaves and masses of plants. He went on to say that his colony, as that is the name of a group of beavers, built the dam to protect themselves from predators.

Mason asked what he and his new found friend could do to help. "Please could you find items for the gaps?" replied a baby beaver, or as they are officially known, a kit. The boys wandered off in search of the supplies needed. Each time they returned their arms were laden with large amounts of the aforementioned supplies needed. Every time they came back with their arms full it felt like it was only seconds later and their arms were magically empty ready for the next load.

Mason began to realise that this was going to be a huge task, he thought that maybe more bodies would make their job a little easier. Mason recalled what the robins had said, without warning he let out a mighty whistle so loud that the whole colony stopped what they were doing and stared at him. The poor kits had been so startled that they ran to hide with their front paws covering their ears. "Sorry," said a shamefaced Mason, he felt so embarrassed at how he had scared everyone when all he really wanted to do was help. "I thought it might be a good idea to call for reinforcements." by way of an explanation.

A blush of robins swooped down landing wherever they could. One landed on Hugo's head, another on Mason's shoulder and asked how they could be of assistance. Mason asked if they would not mind helping them all by collecting items for the beavers dam. One robin bowed its little head, "Anything for you Master Mason," he tweeted and flew from Mason's shoulder. With all these helpers the beavers soon had their dam complete. A loud cheer went up as the final gap was filled. Hugo admired the dam wishing he could build something this strong and secure at home to keep his predators, the bullies, away.

Hugo and Mason gave each other a hug, they felt a little awkward though so jumped apart rather quickly looking red faced as they walked away from each other. The robins showed their flying prowess and acrobatic skills as the beavers prepared a feast for one and all. Everyone enjoyed the food, all relaxing together after their hard day of work. They sang, danced and had lots of fun. Hugo joined in by telling a few jokes making everyone laugh. Eventually the fun, frolics and festivities ended as everyone snuggled down for the night.

Mason and Hugo felt safer sleeping with these animals nearby, even though they had not told each other this. As Mason was making himself comfortable on a bed of moss, he spotted one of the beavers approaching him. The beavers stopped and bowed his head, he slid his paw towards Mason.

Under his paw there was an orange pebble, Mason looked down at the pebble as the beaver said "Please keep this pebble safe Master Mason, as you will surely need it later." Mason remembered that these exact words had been spoken by the robin about the red pebble! Mason was now certain he had to keep these pebbles as safe as he possibly could, he was sure he would find out why soon enough. The orange pebble from the beavers was placed inside his pocket where the red pebble, from the robins, already resided.

That night Mason had the strangest dream. He dreamt of a young girl with long flowing hair and the greenest eyes Mason had ever seen. The girl looked very sad. She appeared to be sweeping and humming to herself. Mason thought he had heard the song before somewhere, but he could not quite reach the memory.

The girl hummed a haunting lament whilst doing her chores. All of a sudden the humming stopped and she looked up as though startled by something. "Please, come and find me, save me from this life! I can be found at Chips cottage," she wailed whilst still staring ahead. Mason felt as though she was looking directly at him, he jumped awake. Who was this girl? Who was Chip? Where could he find the cottage? Was he the one she was calling out too? And was he the one that was meant to save her? These thoughts whirled around his head, was this a dream or a premonition? Mason wondered if he would meet this girl whilst wandering through the forest.

Once morning broke, Mason told Hugo all about the strange dream, his eyes glazing over when he talked about the girl. Hugo began to laugh "Ohhhhhhh Mason is in Luuuuurrrvvvvee," he teased.

Mason slapped Hugo on the back "No I am not! Shut up!." Neither boy meant any harm though, they were just being boys, they both crumpled to the ground in a fit of giggles.

Chapter 6
CHIP AND MARISSA

Here are the last of the children we need to meet, then we can continue our adventures. Chip had always felt invisible, not because of how thin he was, but because he had been ignored most of his life. At school, he sat at the back of the classroom never being seen, or getting picked by the teacher. At home he had been left alone, literally.

His parents had full-time jobs, many a night working over-time. They no longer left little notes for the son telling him where his dinner was. In the beginning he had enjoyed the freedom, but one night he fell ill. There had been no one there to tend to him or bring him water or administer medicine.

Chip learned how to look after himself from that point onwards, preparing food, taking medicine if he needed it, he decided he no longer needed anyone else. It was lonely though, all he wished for was a friend. He spent a lot of time in his bedroom keeping himself occupied by taking things apart, trying to find out how they worked and then putting them back together again. He had even found out that when he played on his games console, if he pressed the buttons of the controller in a certain way, he could manipulate the game he was playing.

His favourite game was "The Enchanted Forest ".
He loved the look of the countryside, the trees, even the animals made him smile. He decided he was going to try pressing his controller buttons to see if he could get inside the game and

he was in!

Chip whooped with joy. He was free of his parents, his room, maybe now he would be able to find the friends he so longed for, someone to laugh and play with. Months passed and Chip had not found any other boy or girl anywhere in the forest. He was sat, bored one evening when his brain began to whirr with an idea. If he could get himself into the game, then would that not mean he could get someone else into the game too?

 He could barely contain his excitement as his fingers set to work on a code for his mission. Then he began to think, if he could bring in one person then it stood to reason he could bring in more and more and more!

The boy laughed at what he felt was his most brilliant idea yet. But, all was not perfect, he had brought in a girl! The idea of this alone made him shudder. She would not want to play the games that he liked. Which was a very unfair judgement to make, as we all know both girls and boys can play together if they want too. Marissa, as this was the girl's name, hated this new world and she hated Chip for taking her to a strange place where her grandfather was not. She missed him terribly. Chip had not been able to make friends when he had been home, so he really did not know how to treat a friend.

What Chip really would have liked was for Marissa to sit with him at breakfast time, but instead of asking Marissa politely, he would bark out orders. Marissa would make Chip his breakfast, but each time he hoped that she would sit with him she would simply place his food on the table, then take her leave and go outside to the chickens.

She preferred to sit with the birds because they did not boss her around, like the boy did. Marissa refused to call Chip by his name, she would just nod at him with her eyes full of sorrow. Chip wanted to ask Marissa to be his friend and help with the cottage, but each time he tried it came out sounding like a command. The more Chip tried to be nice, the worse he sounded until he just gave up trying.

He decided that if she did not like him then he would not like her either! He thought that having someone close meant they were your friend, you did not really have to like them right? Even though Chip said he did not like Marissa he would not let her leave either. Marissa cried herself to sleep every night, weeping for the grandfather that she missed terribly. She wept for his little shop and she wept worrying about whether she would ever see her family again.

Every night Marissa would hum a tune that her and her grandfather sang together at bedtime, eventually she would fall asleep. She once dreamt of a small boy with blonde hair and an amazing smile. It seemed as though this boy could see her in her dreams! "Please, come and find me, save me from this life! I can be found at Chips cottage." she pleaded. Had the boy heard her? Marissa could only hope and pray that he had.

Chapter 7
THE RABBIT AND THE TRAP

"Help! Please someone help me!" The desperate cry echoed through the forest. The boys froze mid step upon hearing it "Where are you?" Mason shouted, cupping his hands to his mouth in the hope of making his voice heard as far away as possible.

"Trapped under the horse chestnut tree." came a reply. Hugo began to look, but because he had spent so much time in his bedroom, he had no clue as to what type of tree he should be looking for. If you're not sure, here are some tips to help you identify one. The leaves look like a hand with five to seven pointed serrated leaflets spreading from the central stem. When the leaf falls from the tree branch the stalk leaves a scar on the branch that resembles an inverted horse shoe with nail holes, conkers come from the horse chestnut tree. When they are on the tree, the conker is surrounded by a spiky green casing. Mason had learned about the tree when he had earned his nature badge with the boy scouts. Which was lucky for Mason and the voice that was trapped.

Mason found the tree and looked at the base of the trunk, he could see a knotted tangle of tatty muddled ropes. Underneath the rope, Mason could see something small wriggling trying to escape. A twitching nose appeared first, closely followed by the cute face of a fluffy grey rabbit.

"I am stuck, I am afraid I have wriggled into a knotty mess and cannot free myself." the little face looked up and beseeched "Can one of you please help me?"

"me! me! I can free you!" shouted Hugo, lunging towards the knotty mess with his arms outstretched.

"Aaargh!" scared the rabbit, pooping itself with fear. Mason told Hugo that they needed to be very careful and quiet so as to not scare the already frightened rabbit more.

"I am so sorry," replied Hugo. He bent towards the rabbit who was shaking with fear. Looking all around the rabbit and then behind it, Hugo pointed at something, they were small round little brown berry looking shapes. "Raisins!" he exclaimed, rubbing his tummy that had just let out a huge growl of hunger. Mason stifled a giggle "Oh Hugo, they are not raisins! That is rabbit poop you silly thing," Hugo walked off grumbling.

"Well they looked like raisins to me," and went to sit and sulk under a nearby tree. Mason sat beside the rabbit patiently trying to untangle the knotty mess.

"You know I would not be in this mess," began the rabbit "but I have been trying to watch my weight, Spinach is low in calories you know," Mason nodded, silently continuing with the tangles. The rabbit went on with the one sided conversation, "It has always been my dream to appear on the front cover of Bunny Weekly, for me to do this I need to stay in shape and keep my girly figure." Mason could not help but think how amazing it was that even rabbits had dreams and ambitions. Masons' fingers were beginning to go a little numb, he realised he needed help.

"I will be back in a moment," he said, walking back down towards the beavers dam.

Once he got there he explained to the beavers his dilemma and asked if they might help him, the beavers agreed sending their best "chewers" for the job. Mason and the beavers returned to the ensnared rabbit and set to work. Mason would gently pull at the netting that was too close to the rabbits skin so that the beavers might be able to get their teeth in there and chew through the rope safely. With them all working as a team, the rabbit was finally freed. "Thank you so much," said the grateful bunny. The beavers turned to Mason and bid him farewell and returned to the river bank and home. The rabbit skipped around gleefully, "thank you, thank you, please wait here I have something for you," she said, hopping away only to return moments later.

The rabbit gave Mason a beautiful sunshine yellow pebble.

"Please take this as a token of my gratitude," "Thank you," said Mason, placing the pebble in his pocket alongside the red and orange ones that were already there. One red pebble One orange pebble One yellow pebble What could it all mean? How intriguing!

Chapter 8
MILKING OF THE COWS

Mason and Hugo left the rabbit happily munching on the spinach. Continuing along their journey, Mason wondered what would happen next? Where would this adventure take them? Hugo was only wondering where his next meal would come from, he was hungry and his stomach kept complaining at him with a loud growl. They had not gone much further when they could hear mooing in the distance. Hugo began to lick his lips. Surely he was not hoping to eat a whole cow? Thought Mason, shuddering at the idea.

Of course, Hugo was not doing that, hunger can do strange things to a boy, Hugo did not hear mooing he was hearing the word "Moon", Moon pie was his favourite, all that chewy marshmallow surrounded by biscuit, coated in yummy chocolate. Hugo was smacking his lips, describing what Moon pie was to Mason who thought it sounded very much like the wagon wheels he would eat in the U.K.

Mason handed Hugo an apple in an attempt to hopefully satisfy his friend's hunger.

Hugo eyed the apple distastefully and begrudgingly took a bite.

The boys walked towards the sound. In a field stood three brown and white cows, all mooing mournfully. They seemed to be struggling to walk, their udders were very saggy and large. Mason knew that cows produced milk and he thought they might need milking. One of the cows approached the boys, her beautiful brown eyes staring at them. She fluttered her huge eyelashes and asked "Is she coming?"
"Who?" queried Mason.

The bovine beast, that's a cow to me and you, told the boys about a girl that used to come and milk them, but they were worried as they had not seen the girl for quite some time. If they were not milked soon then they could all become very sick. The cows were not aware that the young girl was being kept against her will and would not be able to come to their aid.

Chip did not know about the cows, he had been keeping a very close eye on Marissa lately. Mason wondered whether Hugo knew how to milk them. He was doubtful because Hugo had already told him about how much time he spent in his bedroom. There was another problem, What would they put the milk in?

Searching around for something that could hold the milk proved futile, so they decided to search further afield promising the cows they would return as soon as they had found a suitable receptacle. As the boys were searching, Hugo made up a little song which went a little something like this………..

A bucket for the milk,
milk from a cow,
I need a bucket,
then I can drink some milk.

It was clear to Mason that Hugo was neither a poet nor a singer. Mason joined in with the singing as they continued to walk and search, they came to a clearing. Walking towards it they could see that something was wrong. What should have been a beautiful area to sit, was covered with litter and sweet wrappers with mouldy food strewn all around. Mason shuddered at the mess. He felt this might be another test for him. To clear the area or not? What would you do? Well, Mason was always being told by his mum and dad that he should never leave litter, he should always clear up after himself especially when outside, as the litter not only looked bad, but it could be a problem to animals too.

Animals could get tangled up in plastics or loose wrappers, really hurting themselves in the process and he did not want to be responsible for that! "This mess must be cleared!" he exclaimed.

Hugo shook his head and tutted "Have you forgotten about the cows already?"

Mason had not forgotten, but if this place was not cleared then more animals would need help. So, that meant if they cleared the mess then maybe just maybe they could prevent that and be able to get home. Hugo was not so enthusiastic about clearing up. He held his nose because of the smell and everything he picked up was by a finger and thumb pincer motion. The boys had almost finished when Mason spotted a tub half hidden in some long grass. "Look!" he shouted "This is perfect for the milk."

Hugo jumped up and down with excitement and relief. Excitement because a bucket of some kind had been found and relief at not having to do anymore stinky cleaning up. The pair made their way back to the cows. They were very hot and sweaty by now, but they knew that the trio of cows needed them. Their next problem was to figure out how to milk cows. Both boys stood staring at the tub, then at the cows, "What do we do now?" asked Hugo. Mason shrugged his shoulders. One of the cows stepped forward. "You look confused" she said.

"We are," they replied. "We're not sure how to do this." The cow explained what needed to be done. "Place the tub below my udders then get yourself into a comfortable position." Hugo did as he was told. "Place your hand at the top of my udder and gently pull downwards from the base to the teat." It took Hugo a couple of attempts. The cow was trying to help with comments like "too gentle," or "owwwwwww too much!" Finally Hugo got the hang of it, milking all three cows in next to no time. He felt rather proud of his accomplishments.

"Bravo Hugo!" Mason clapped his hands with a look of pride on his face. Once more the cows approached, one of them had something sticking out of her mouth. It was green and round. Another pebble!

"Thank you for milking us, here is a token of our gratitude." "What is it with all these pebbles?" Hugo was exasperated. "I'm not sure, but I feel we need to find out," replied Mason. He placed the pebble into his pocket where it made a clacking sound as it hit the other three.

Chapter 9
A WOLF CUB

The boys began to walk once more singing Hugo's silly milk song and laughing.

A bucket for the milk,
milk from a cow,
I need a bucket,
then I can drink some milk.

Mason thought he heard something so he stood still and cupped his hand to his ear. Hugo was still walking and singing, oblivious that he was now walking alone. "Shhhhhh," whispered Mason, "I thought I heard something." Both boys were now standing, with one hand each cupped to an ear as the breeze whistled through the trees, the leaves gently rustling together. "There it is again." It was faint at first, barely a whimper. The boys tiptoed quietly forward with a hand still resting beside their ear. They stepped then listened, listened then stepped trying to trace where this sad sound was coming from. Scanning the area Hugo spotted what looked like a small wall with poles on either side and another pole balanced on top. It looked a little like a goal post with some rope wrapped around the uppermost pole. Stepping closer they heard the whimpering sound again. "It sounds like it is coming from over there," Hugo said as he pointed towards the strange construction. The pair rushed forward. They realised it was not a wall after all, but a dilapidated well.

The well was no longer in use as the winding handle that lowered the bucket down was broken. At the end of the rope there was no bucket attached, just frayed tatters at the end. Going to the edge of the well Mason carefully leaned over to peer inside. All he could see was darkness. He cupped his hands to his mouth and yelled "Helloooooooo, loooooooo, loooooo, ooooooo," the well echoed back.

A disembodied voice floated from the darkness. "Please can you help me? I fell down this well and I can not get out. My mum and dad will be so worried about me." The boys exchanged glances, a mum and dad? Here? Maybe if they helped then this person's parents would help them to return home. Mason and Hugo scrabbled for the rope and began to pull with all their might, but nothing moved! They feared that all the walking they had done had maybe sapped their strength. Realising they couldn't do it alone Mason dropped the rope and ran off in the direction of the cows. Leaving Hugo to stand guard.

Mason found the cows and quickly explained that he needed help. The cows were more than happy to help now that they were comfortable again. They knew they could have fallen ill without help from the boys. They felt it was only right to repay them in kind.

The cows followed Mason back along the trail to the well. Hugo had been sitting beside the wall, resting and munching on an apple when he spotted the return of Mason with three brown and white cows following behind him. Hugo jumped

up to greet them. He grabbed the rope and handed it to the first cow, who in turn passed it back. The three cows from the rescue party stood beside the rope, one behind the other with Mason at the back.

"HEAVE HO, HEAVE HO," commanded Hugo. All five pulled fiercely.

The rope began to move bringing the trapped person ever closer to the top of the wall and their freedom.
Hugo gasped and fell backwards as two huge yellow eyes appeared, followed by a large mouth with fangs and a lolling tongue. A wolf cub jumped from the well to the ground. He was so happy to be free that he gave a howl of delight, not noticing that his rescuers had frozen with fear. The boys had no clue that when the wolf cub howled he had alerted his parents to his whereabouts.

The cows nodded towards the boys bidding them farewell whilst eyeing the cub warily, they turned and went on their return journey. The last cow disappeared from view. Two gigantic wolves leapt into the clearing beside the well. Their hackles risen, snarling and drooling as they slowly, menacingly stepped towards the shaking boys.

Hugo was so frightened that he let out a little toot from his behind. He grabbed Mason by the arm and whispered "Oh my word! I think I am going to raisin myself!" Mason thought back to the rabbit. If he had not been so scared he might have laughed at Hugo's strange sense of humour. The boys feared that this would be the end of their journey. But to their surprise the wolf cub jumped in front of the two giant wolves. "No Mama, no Papa, these who-mans saved me!" Mason thought it was rather cute to be called a "who-man." He smiled shyly at the wolves, hoping his extraordinary smile would work on them too. The wild beasts stepped towards the boys then they stopped and bowed deeply. Wolves mate for life, their families being so important to them that they would forgo what looked like a delicious titbit or two in exchange for their sons safety. The larger of the wolves spoke. "Thank you for saving my son who-mans." Is this the name all wolves gave us? Thought Mason.

The wolf continued "We owe you our gratitude. Until our debt to you is paid we are your servants." The other wolf now stepped forward, she slipped her paw towards Mason and Hugo. When she retracted her paw, there on the ground was a blue pebble.

 "Take this pebble, keep it safe, you might need it later." she said. Mason bent over and carefully picked up the pebble and placed it in his pocket.

Chapter 10
CONFRONTING CHIP

When Chip first gained entry into the game he realised a few things. Firstly, he would need somewhere to live and sleep. As luck would have it he found the perfect place. A two bedroomed cottage with all the usual rooms, living room,

kitchen, etc.. It also had a fence with bushes surrounding it and a chicken coop plus an outdoor toilet. Secondly, he needed food. Apples were all around, but he wanted more.

Chip caught some hens, he could now add eggs to his food source. Thirdly, he was becoming bored and lonely. That is when he had an idea to bring in others so he could make friends.

He had found Marissa was a difficult girl to befriend. The problem was twofold, Chip had no idea how to be friends with anyone. He had always struggled with that. Also Marissa was so upset that she had been brought to a place she did not know and had been taken from her best friend, her grandfather!

Chip felt he had tried his very best to be friendly, but every time he spoke to Marissa it sounded like the boy was commanding his "friend" to do something instead of asking. The pair fell into a routine by default. Chip wanted breakfast so Marissa made it.

When he sat eating he hoped that she would join him. He wanted someone to talk to, someone to laugh with. Each morning Marissa would place a breakfast in front of "the boy", that is what she had taken to calling him, she had promised herself she would never say his name. (She thought that if she did the things he asked then maybe he would let her go home). Once the food had been placed in front of him she would go outside to the fresh air and feed the chickens. Marissa would take a seat beside the coop, nibble on her food and chat to the hens, telling them all about her amazing grandfather. Sometimes she was able to sneak off and milk some cows she had found in a field. She would then drink the milk without telling "the boy" knowing it gave her an inner revenge for him trapping her.

Each day became harder for both Chip and Marissa. Chip longing for friendship, Marissa longing for freedom and home. Marissa would while away her day with the hens, chatting with them. She would watch them tilt their heads as though they were listening to every word she spoke. She had just placed a plate of eggs in front of the boy when a commotion outside caught her attention. Grabbing her shawl she ran outside to investigate. The chickens were squawking and for good reason. Two sets of eyes could be seen glaring at the hens from the bushes. The bushes began to rustle as the wolves slowly crept forward, their mouths hanging open with rivulets of saliva dangling down. They looked very hungry. Marissa knew she had to do something to save the chickens. She grabbed a rake that conveniently lay close by.

Pulling from the very depths of her soul she let out a shriek and ran towards the chickens. Marissa had been hoping that the noise she made would have been enough to scare the beasts away, but alas that was not the case. The wolves just snarled and took another step closer.

Marissa stood in front of the chicken coop with rake in hand, as ready as she would ever be to defend her friends. The chickens had become just that to the lonely sad girl, chicken friends. Marissa stood waiting to fight the wolves if she had too, little did she know that her scream from earlier had been heard by two boys. Upon hearing this blood curdling scream the boys began to run as fast as they could towards the sound. They had never heard a scream like it but they knew that whoever made this sound was desperate for help.

They ran through tree branches, bushes, overgrown grass and anything else that might be in their way. At last they got through the wall of greenery and there standing before them was a scared looking young girl with a rake in her hand. To the left of her were the two wolf parents, who Mason and Hugo had come across earlier, snarling and growling. The boys ran full speed towards the wolves, once they reached them they began to whisper to them whilst still trying to catch their breath. Marissa could not understand what was happening.

Were these boys in cahoots with the wolves? Marissa had not heard the exchange of words between wolves and boy, so she continued her warrior-like stance with the rake still held aloft in her hand. Mason moved hesitantly towards her. Marissa was deep in thought, how had these boys managed to find her? Were they here to save her? What had they said to the wolves? All of these thoughts were rushing around her mind. Mason touched the girls' arm lightly, bringing her out of her confusing thoughts. He introduced himself and went on to explain how the boys were searching for a way home.

Hearing this Marissa was filled with hope and a longing to join them. "Could you take me with you?" she asked. "Noooooooooooo!" screamed Chip from the cottage doorway. He had been watching the whole drama unfold, just watching in stunned silence. Marissa dropped the rake in shock when she heard Chips' scream. The infuriated boy stomped towards the trio, anger vibrating through his every fibre, his eyes boring into them one by one. "What are you doing here? What do you want?" demanded Chip. Even though Hugo was the biggest of them all, he stepped behind Mason shaking with fear. Hugo pushed Mason forward to deal with this screaming angry looking boy.

"Hi, my name is Mason " he said and extended his hand in friendship, he really hoped that no one would spot how much his hand was shaking.
"Chip," came the terse reply. Where have I heard that name before? Pondered Mason.
"Please, let me leave with these boys." came a quiet request. It was Marissa begging to leave with tears in her eyes.

A thought began to form in Masons' mind. Was this the girl in his dream? Was she the one he was meant to save?
Something had to be done, but what?
"You're my friend!" said Chip. "You should want to stay with me, why don't you want to stay with me?" he whined.
"Why would I want to stay with you?! Friends do not steal people away from their family, they do not force you to work for them all day" retorted Marissa indignantly.

"No, I will not allow you to leave" shouted Chip as he grabbed the girl by the wrist and began dragging her towards the cottage.
"Chip! Leave her alone" demanded Mason.

"Pfft, I will do no such thing. She is MY friend and she will stay with me" Chip turned his back letting the boys know that as far as he was concerned it was the end of the conversation.

Chapter 11
HUGO THE HERO

Hugo had been listening to the confrontation between
Mason, Chip and Marissa, he could not believe what Chip was
saying. He began to shake in anger. His new found bravery
and indignation overtaking his usual sense of fear.
"ENOUGH!" he shouted, stepping towards Chip. As he spoke
a beam of light shone down on him, shimmering across his
body making it glow with an ethereal beauty. "I have heard
enough!"

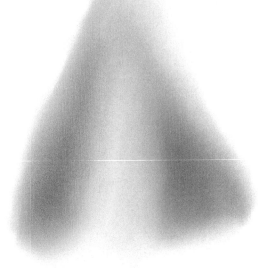

Chip, Marissa and Mason all turned towards the usually placid boy. "You are a bully Chip, there is no other word to describe you! Do you know how it feels to be bullied?" Chip stared at Hugo, his mouth opening and closing, completely flabbergasted at his tirade, no words would come out.

"Well I know, I know only too well. It makes you feel small, insignificant, unliked and lonely. It makes you feel like anything you do or say is not good enough, that you're not good enough. It makes you feel like screaming, crying, wanting to hide from everyone and everything. Do YOU like making people feel like they are not worth anything? Does it make YOUR life better by doing it!" Hugo heaved a sigh of relief at finally being able to speak out about how bullying makes you feel. It felt exhilarating.

He felt the strength of his convictions fill him with this new found bravery. Chip hung his head in shame.
"We should be trying to make people feel better about themselves, not worse! I finally see that I am good enough, I am kind, caring and worthy of friendship and nothing you or anyone else can say or do will ever, EVER make me feel bad about myself again!"

Chip let go of Marissa. He stood with tears in his eyes. "What have I done?" he cried, falling to the ground and covering his face with his hands. "I'm so sorry Marissa," he sobbed. Everyone was so amazed and shocked by Hugo and his bravery that they all froze on the spot. Hugo took a step towards the weeping boy placing a hand on his shoulder, he said "Do you promise to never treat anyone like this again?" Chip stood and solemnly vowed "cross my heart, hope to fly, stick a cupcake in my eye."

Marissa walked forward and did something she thought she would never do, she gave Chip a hug, she laughed and said "I have never heard a promise said like that before, but, I forgive you." Chip could not believe how kind everyone was being. He had been so awful to Marissa but everyone seemed to want to forgive him. Mason felt a little left out so walked over and joined the embrace. His hand brushed against Marissa's, it was as though a bolt of lightning struck the pair. They both exclaimed "It's you! From my dream."
"What?" Said Mason.
"I dreamt of you!" Marissa declared.
"I dreamt of you too!" Mason admitted in shock.
"WOW that's weird" they cried in unison.

The group sat down to try and work out what their next move should be. Mason took the pebbles from his pocket, "I have these, I feel we need them, but I have no clue why." he said whilst showing them to everyone.

 Marissa took a pebble and placed it on the ground, then took another and did the same thing. She mumbled "red, orange, yellow, green, blue" she smiled "Do you see it?"
"See what?" asked a puzzled Hugo

"These are the colours of the rainbow," Marissa said, putting her hand inside her pocket. "Have you heard the rhyme?" She asked "Richard of York gave battle in vain."

"What are you babbling about?" scoffed Hugo, rolling his eyes.

"The first letter of each word represents a colour from the rainbow and their order. Red first, then orange so on and so forth," Marissa remembered that she too had received a pebble when she first came to this strange place; she had kept it safe ever since, with no real reason as to why she had. She pulled her hand from her pocket and produced her pebble, it was indigo in colour.

"What does that have to do with anything?" Hugo questioned
"Maybe, if we find the final colour, we will find out" replied Mason.

"There's one more? What colour is that one?" asked Hugo, getting rather frustrated with all these pebbles and colours.

"Violet" Chip replied, he was still feeling terrible about what he had done, and wanted to try to make amends. "Come on, let's find the final pebble." The foursome stood up, cheered and began to walk again, not really knowing where they were going or what would happen next.

Chapter 12
THE FINAL PEBBLE

The group of adventurers were all daydreaming as they walked. Mason was wondering where the next pebble would be found. Hugo was hoping the pebble would be found inside a huge pie, he would happily step forward for that task! Marissa was hoping she would be able to see her grandfather again soon. Chip's heart was weighing heavy. Something had been playing on his mind since Hugo's speech. He was not sure he wanted or deserved to go home. He felt that no one would have missed him, and that his life was worth more being the forgotten one and staying where he was right now. "I have decided that I do not want to go home," he announced "Oh no, please don't say that!" cried Marissa

"I can't go back, I had no life at home. I don't think anyone will have even missed me and I feel ashamed by the way I have treated you." Chip admitted. "I have fun here, even if it is a little lonely, maybe one of you would like to stay with me?" He asked, hoping that one of them would say yes. Mason, Hugo and Marissa felt sorry for Chip and it saddened them that he felt this way, but none of them could imagine never seeing their families again.

They decided to take a rest as their hunger and fatigue was taking over. Sitting under the apple trees that were scattered all around the forest, the children each picked an apple and began to eat. All except Hugo, he picked two.

Marissa spotted a field full of daisies, she finished her apple and decided she would like to make some daisy chains. One for each of her friends. She stood up and walked towards them, little did she realise she was being followed. When Chip saw Marissa leave he decided to follow her so that he could apologise to her once more over his despicable behaviour.

Marissa sat down amongst the daisies, picked them and placed them onto her skirt for safe keeping. As she went to pick another flower she saw a bee laying on its back. The bee was barely moving, occasionally kicking its legs feebly and buzzing. Then it would stay still, appearing to be catching its breath only to start the whole procedure again. Marissa had never been scared of bees. She knew they would not sting unless they really had too.

Dear reader, just because Marissa is not scared of bees and likes to pick them up does not mean that you should. Marissa knows what she is doing, you on the other hand might not and you could end up being stung, so please please do not do what Marissa is doing. Once a bee stings, the sting stays in your skin, ripping away from the bee's body, ultimately killing it.

Marissa whispered "do not be afraid little bee, I will save you," she crouched down and gently picked the bee up.

"Kill it! Stomp on it!" screamed Chip making Marissa jump.

"Chip, why would I kill a poor defenceless creature?" she asked.

"It will sting you! They are horrible creatures, Kill it!, KILL IT!" Cried Chip running around waving his arms in the most bizarre way. As Marissa watched Chip leaping around she could not help but laugh at such a funny dance. The bee was safely sitting on Marissas' hand, watching the boy doing his crazy dance. Chip had always been afraid of bees, but watching Marissa calmly holding it gave Chip a little confidence to take a closer look. Chip felt so brave that he asked "May I hold the bee please?"

He glanced down at the bee and said "If that would be okay with you too little bee" Marissa gently placed the bee onto Chips' outstretched palm. He stared closely at the bee, it felt like there was nothing there. He started to feel rather silly for being scared of such a tiny creature. "Oh beautiful bee, I'm so sorry for what I have done to your kind in the past, but I promise I will never harm another bee as long as I live." Marissa started to tell Chip how wonderful bees were. They pollinate three quarters of the worlds' important crops. But they are under threat from being sprayed and killed with pesticides. The bee listened intently to this exchange of promises and facts, she cleared her little throat and buzzed "Thank you Marissa for knowing so much about us." Marissa blushed with pride.

The bee looked at Chip, "Master Chip, the Queen Bee has announced that the forest and all who reside in it need you to care for us, nurture us, feed us and keep us safe. She feels that you are very misunderstood, like us. Please will you stay and become our guardian?" Pleaded the bee. Chip was astounded by the request. He felt a curious warmth flow through his body that he had never felt before. A feeling of pride and finally a feeling of belonging. "I would be honoured," he replied, bowing his head in gratitude and respect.

The bee turned to both children and asked them to follow her to the apiary. Following along Chip whispered "What's an apiary?" Marissa explained that it was all the beehives together in one place. When they arrived at the apiary the bee asked Marissa to place her hand just inside one of the beehives as there was a gift hidden inside. Marissa bravely did as she was asked, she felt something small, cold and round. Pulling her hand out, she saw it was another coloured pebble. "Please take this violet pebble as a token of our gratitude, farewell Marissa and safe journey." Chip and Marissa waved goodbye to the bee and excitedly headed back to Mason and Hugo.

Chapter 13
A SIGN

Mason was still sitting under the apple tree trying to work out what it all meant. How could he get home? How could he get everyone else home? As he was thinking, he picked up a stick and began doodling on the soft ground. "Oh, an infinity sign," Marissa said as she returned from her encounter with the bee and saw Masons' doodle.

"A what?" asked Mason. "I thought it looked like a number eight on its' side!"

"No, my mum showed me this sign when I was little. It is definitely an infinity sign." she said. Mason thought he had seen this sign before, but he could not recollect from where.

"Let's review what we have." the children gathered around. Mason, once again, removed the pebbles from his pocket.

1 x Red pebble from the robins
1 x Orange pebble from the beavers
1 x Yellow pebble from the rabbit
1 x Green pebble from the cows
1 x Blue pebble from the wolf cub
1 x Indigo pebble from Marissa

"But what does it all mean?" asked Hugo

"There's still one missing," smirked Marissa

"That's all I have," sighed Mason. Marissa giggled as she reached into her pocket pulling out the final pebble, she placed it on the ground beside the others. 1 x violet pebble from the bees. The foursome stared at the pebbles. What did they need to do, they all wondered?

Hugo pointed at each one of the pebbles and said the rhyme Marissa had said earlier. "Richard of York gave battle in vain" he said, then held his hands up into the air as though beseeching the sky to help. Nothing happened. Hugo shrugged, "It was worth a try," he said.

Marissa was the next to try. She placed the pebbles in order but she arched them so as to resemble a rainbow. Nothing happened.

Chip stepped forward. "Third time lucky." He placed the pebbles in the infinity sign shape that Mason had drawn. Again nothing happened.

Marissa, Hugo and Chip all looked up at Mason, hopefully he would know what to do. Mason looked at the pebbles then back at the three expectant faces. Where have I seen these colours and this pattern before, he thought to himself.

Mason felt his leg begin to shake. He felt something in his pocket, was it another pebble? He was sure that he had emptied his pocket of them all. Placing his hand inside he felt something cool and round, it was vibrating. "What the…….. How did that get there?" It was the controller from his console! On the controller there were seven small indentations around what he now knew was the infinity sign. "I wonder," he whispered. Picking up the red pebble he carefully placed it into one of the holes, it was a perfect fit. The controller vibrated once more and the red stone began to glow. Hugo picked up the orange pebble and placed it into the controller, it began to glow alongside the red pebble. Marissa quickly grabbed the yellow pebble, shaking with anticipation as she placed it onto the controller.

Three glowing pebbles! Chip picked up the green pebble, but before he placed the pebble he said with determination. "Guys, I am not coming with you. I have been asked to stay here and become guardian of this land. I want to do the right thing, I want to stay and help. But I do wish you well on your journey." He put the pebble into its place on the controller. With tears in his eyes he turned to walk away.

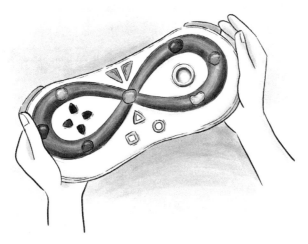

Marissa, Hugo and Mason grabbed him and pulled the boy into a huge bear hug. "We will miss you!" they cried. "I will miss you too, you have taught me so much, but I am needed here." Chip gave the trio a smile, stood up straight and with his head held high walked away. The three remaining children each picked up one of the three pebbles left. "Here goes nothing," Mason said as they all placed a pebble onto the controller. Each child had their hand on the controller when a myriad of colours exploded from it, wrapping them in a cocoon of rainbow flashes.

WHOOSH

Chapter 14
MARISSA HOME AT LAST

Marissa stumbled forward dizzily, her arms outstretched in an attempt to keep her balance. She did not open her eyes for a moment trying to steady herself. She heard a familiar voice. "Little bit?" the voice said. Was she dreaming? Could this really be her grandfather? Marissa slowly opened her eyes, her heart thumping in her chest.

Grandfather Alan watched his granddaughter appear out of nowhere, as though out of the very ether itself. He could not believe his eyes! Could this be real? Was he dreaming? Alan fell to his knees, arms reaching towards Marissa crying "Little bit, oh my little bit your home." Marissa ran with wild abandon into her grandfather's arms, to safety, to home.

Chapter 15
MASON AND HUGO
HOME AT LAST

Mason stumbled forward dizzily, looking around trying to find his bearings. He was back in his bedroom. Mason was so relieved to be back in his room, home at last. He ran downstairs into the kitchen where his parents were sat. He wanted to tell them all about his adventure, but there was another person in the kitchen.

The lady's name was Lynda, and she had introduced herself as the new neighbour. She was hoping that Mason might befriend her son. Lynda explained she was very worried about her son as he seemed to spend a lot of time in his room, alone. She was hoping that Mason would be the friend that her son needed to bring him out of his shell. Mason liked making friends so he agreed. He followed Lynda to the house next door to meet this lonely boy.

Hugo stumbled forward dizzily. He too was back in his bedroom. He felt a little sad, unsure as to whether he would be able to leave his bedroom. Whether it would be just like before the adventure, with him too scared to leave. As he was thinking all this through there was a knock on his door.

"Come in," he sighed

"HUGO!" Mason shouted running towards his friend

"OMG, MASON?!"

"What the….?"

"How did……?!

"Did we…..?" Half sentences stumbled from Hugo's mouth. The boys whooped with joy, hugging and laughing.

Chapter 16
TRIO

Mason felt he needed to go and see the old man in the
gaming shop. After all that's how he felt he had ended up in
the adventure. He took Hugo with him. They opened the door
to "Gaming Galore" the tinkle of the overhead bell sounded,
making the owner aware of customers. The boys stood at the
empty counter waiting for the old man to appear. A familiar
face walked through the doorway towards the counter. It was
not the shopkeeper though. "MARISSA!," The boys cried in
unison. Marissa ran around the counter and threw herself into
the boy's open arms, hugging and crying. They were so happy
to be reunited.

They did not hear Marissa's grandfather entering. The old
man stood behind the counter, watching and smiling at the
trios reunion. The three eventually separated from their hug.
The room went quiet, and Alan cleared his throat. "Hello
boys, I am so happy to meet you," looking across to Mason,
the old man nodded and added "Again, I feel that you might
need an explanation as to what happened." The trio quietly
stepped forward, waiting in anticipation for the old man's next
words. "When Marissa went missing, I felt as though my life

was over, my Little bit is one of the only reasons I keep going, along with my shop of course. When you get to my age you find that family means the world to you, even though you love your family, when you're younger. That love deepens the older you get, but, I digress. After Marissa disappeared I kept having these strange dreams, I could hear Little bit singing our favourite song, I could also see a figure in black.

I imagined he must have been the person keeping her there. I also saw the outline of a youngster and something inside me told me that this person, whoever they were, would be Marissa's saviour." At that point Marissa looked at both the boys with appreciation in her eyes.

The Grandfather continued. "I had a vision in that dream, I was to give this saviour 'The Enchanted Forest' game as it was the key to everything, or so I believed or hoped. Thank goodness I listened to my intuition. As soon as you walked into my shop Mason, I just knew that you needed to be given that game, I truly hoped that you would be the right person for the job." The Grandfather took Mason by the hand and looked deep into his eyes as he whispered "Thank you Mason."

He then looked across to Hugo, "Hugo, you are such a brave boy, that bravery will stand you in good stead in the future my young man." Mason and Hugo grinned back at the old man thanking him for starting their whole adventure and their friendship.

Chapter 17
A NEW CHIP

I feel it would be remiss of me to not check back and see how Chip is doing. Of course once Mason, Hugo and Marissa left, Chip felt rather sad. He decided he would venture out investigating the land he had now become the guardian of.

Chip was pleasantly surprised at how friendly and kind all the animals were to him. They worked together to create a safer environment for everyone. He also found plenty of resources for food. Honey from the bees, milk from the cows, nuts and berries brought by the birds. In fact there was so much food that Chip would invite the animals to join him at this smorgasbord of goodies.

Chip became a better person from staying behind, he was more thoughtful, helpful and kind. Sometimes Chip would daydream about going home. Home was different in his dream, with loving parents who cared for him and fed him. Chip would shake himself out of these dreams with a tinge of sadness. He knew he was needed here, he felt he was where he belonged. This was his family for now.

Chapter 18
HUGO STRIKES ONCE MORE

Mason, Hugo and Marissa had the most amazing adventure in 'The Enchanted Forest.' They decided that they would still like to help, even if it was a little closer to home. First things first though, Hugo had decided that he was no longer going to allow himself to be affected by the bullying. He made a few changes, not because of the mean boys that picked on him, he made the changes for himself. A nice haircut (much to his mum's dismay as she loved his curly locks). A new set of clothing (with Marissa's help). New glasses and a subscription to the local gym.

Once back at school Hugo, along with his best friends confronted the bullies. "Your words no longer hurt me. YOU no longer hurt me. I have changed for the better and my hope is that you can too. Do you think you can?! You know that being mean to someone does not make you big or clever.

People do not want to be friends with a bully. They only stick around so that you do not pick on them instead. I think you really need to think about what you are doing and how you can change to be a better person." Mason and Marissa stood a little back from Hugo, but they stood proudly nodding at what their friend was saying.

The bullies hung their heads in shame. The ring leader, a spotty tall boy, stepped forward. Hugo was worried that he might get another beating, to his amazement the bully stuck out his hand and said, "It takes a lot to speak out to me, for that I have a little respect for you, friends?"
"Not yet, maybe one day though," came Hugo's reply as he turned his back on the boys and began to walk away with his head held high. Hugo, Mason and Marissa walked around the corner, Hugo sagged his shoulders and sighed with relief. He was so proud of himself for actually speaking out. Even though it was scary he had managed it with the backing of his friends. Marissa and Mason hugged their friend as they congratulated him on his bravery. Whilst they were in this hugging circle Hugo placed his hand in the middle awaiting the other two hands to join in.

Both Mason and Marissa placed their hands in the centre, almost like a chant they threw their hands in the air and shouted

"INFINITY GANG FOREVER!"

Acknowledgments

Thank you to an amazing artist Stephanie Blake, for really bringing the characters to life. Next time don't doubt yourself! Thank you to Paige Bonner for her lovely little poem/promise. I would also like to take this opportunity to mention some of my family. Hannah (my older daughter) thank you for being the sane one and telling me to read, read and re-read what I had written, without you there would have been a tiny pamphlet full of gobbledygook! Hannah you are my rock. Also I apologise to Jesse and Winnie (my 2 youngest grandchildren) who did not make it into this book, you were both twinkles in your mummy and daddy's eyes (but look out for book 2 because you are in there). Thank you Marissa (my younger daughter) for allowing me to use your name, you make me laugh (most of the time). Daphne, love you mum. Malcolm, thank you for looking after mum. To my dad Alan, gone but not forgotten. Hugo (my coward turned hero) 'woof woof' or 'thank you' in dog language (may you rest in peace) And to an extraordinary boy with an extraordinary smile, my oldest grandson Mason, love you moodle! The biggest most amazing thank you goes out to the three best friends in the world, who have taken many hours to transform this little story for me. My love for you guys knows no bounds, your support has helped me through so much not to mention your patience in creating what you have. You are three very talented ladies Lisa Brum, Kerry Mears and Lianne Wiltshire love you. Finally a huge thank you to you, my amazing reader, I hope you liked it, if you didn't then I am truly sorry and will try to make my next book even better for you.

Thank you all, lots of love,

Suzanna xx

Printed in Great Britain
by Amazon

18261896R00047